This book belongs to:

____

ISBN: 978-1-913339-29-6

A catalogue record of this book is available from the British Library.

THE TOOTH FAIRY

AND THE SUGARPLUM PIXIE

WRITTEN BY
SAMUEL LANGLEY-SWAIN

ILLUSTRATED BY
DAVIDE ORTU

First published in the UK
2022 by Owlet Press
www.owletpress.com

Both Ollie and Grace were fantastic young cooks,
finding sweet treats to make from their recipe books.

They crunched all the cookies, in the hope they would see
some wobbly teeth! But it was not meant to be.

Grace gathered her crumbs up for sweet Little Wren.
She sprinkled them all around the garden but then . . .

Grandpa cleared them away. “Pop some seeds out instead – we shouldn’t feed birds too much sugar,” he said.

“Hmm, sugar . . .” said Ollie. “I wonder . . .” said Grace
with a devious smile spreading over her face.
“A fake tooth,” she said, “to pass fairy inspection.
We’ll get a new coin for our precious collection!”

So the twins very carefully carved a small tooth
from a white sugar lump – only they knew the truth.

But they didn't tell Grandpa. Pretending to sleep,
they cringed as they heard a familiar creep.

"Well, what have you done?" they heard Wensleydale huff.
"You think the tooth fairies will fall for this stuff?"

The twins were embarrassed and knew right away
that the fairies were bound to have something to say.

They reached The Royal Mint and were met by the Chief,
but she didn't look angry – they felt such relief.
"Your teeth are your treasure," the Chief Fairy said.
"But Sugarplum Pixie might trick you instead."

"We fairies look sweet, but this pixie's too much –
obsessed with her ice cream and sweeties and such.

Quite often she's tricksy and works out a plan
to upset all the fairies as much as she can."

“She looks out for children who let their teeth rot
from far too much sugar – they’re easy to spot.
And then in the night, she’ll feed watch-mice some cheese,
making off with the teeth and escaping with ease.”

“I’m sure that your brushing is tickety-boo
and Sugarplum Pixie will not bother you.”
But Ollie and Grace gave a sheepish smile back,
trying hard not to show all their patches of plaque!

You see Ollie and Grace always wanted to rush
each time they squeezed toothpaste out onto a brush.
Their dental routine always felt such a bore;
cleaning teeth was the job that they'd always ignore.

The twins left The Royal Mint with a new point of view towards cleaning their teeth, which was long overdue.

They would brush for two minutes, twice every day –
as part of their mission to stop tooth decay!

At home, they brushed harder than ever before . . .
and out popped two teeth, bouncing onto the floor!

After so much excitement and teeth gleaming white,
the twins smiled at each other as they whispered goodnight.

Look out for more tales, with their treasures and twists;

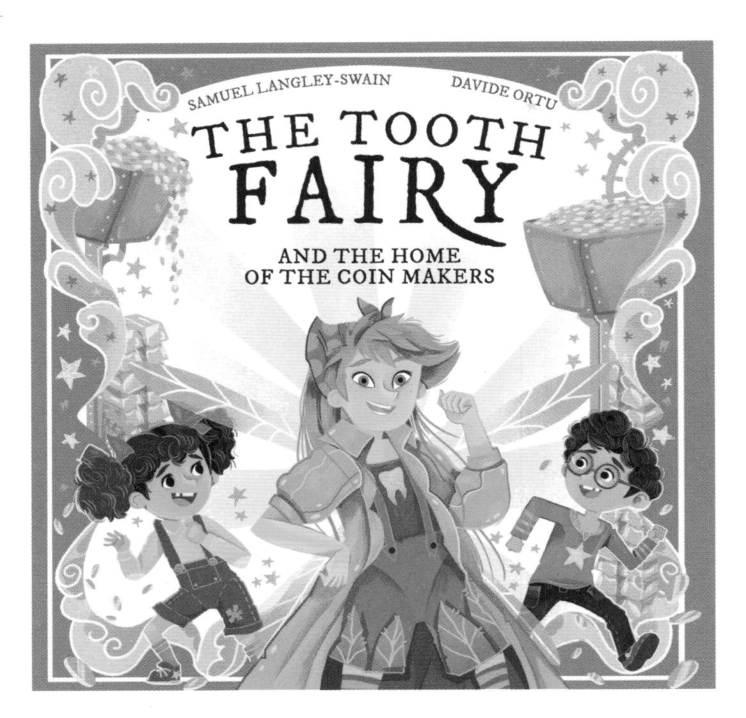

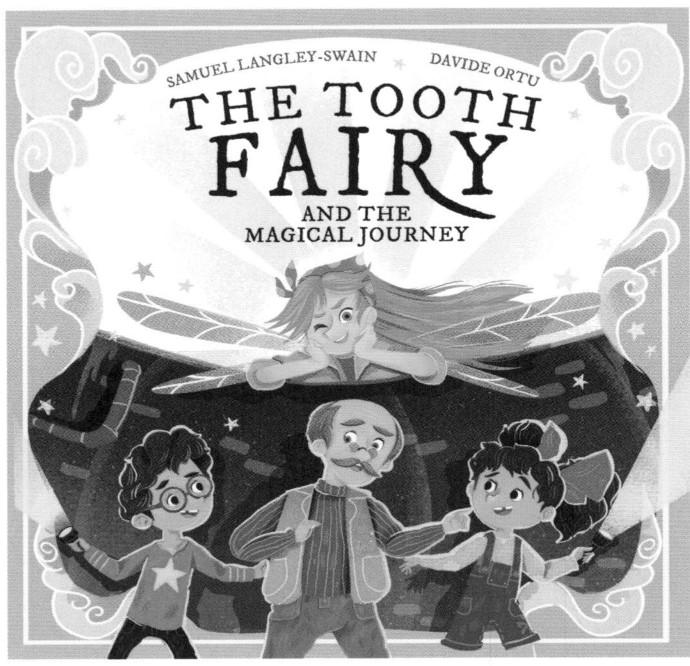

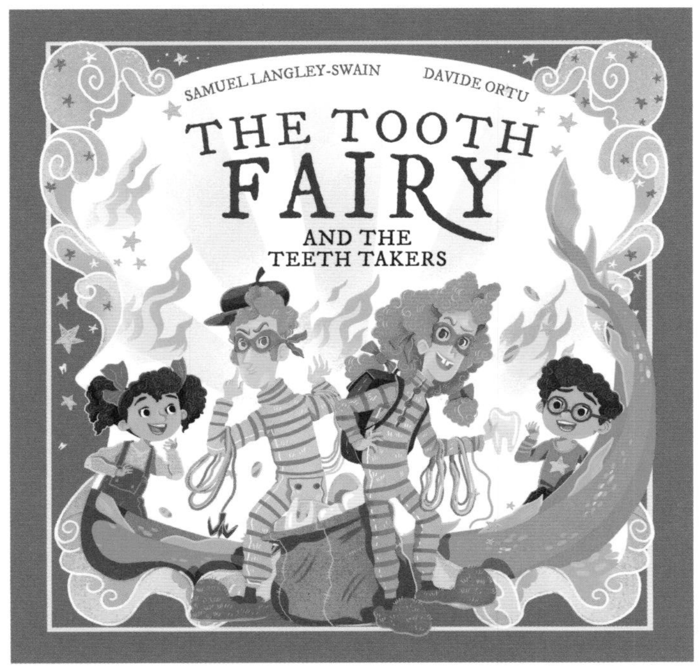

The Royal Mint's magic –
it REALLY exists!
No need to slay dragons.
This book's your invitation.
Just visit our website
for more information!

www.homeofthetoothfairy.com